GOALKEEPER GOOF

My First Graphic Novels are published by Stone Arch Books
151 Good Counsel Drive, P.O. Box 669
Mankato, Minnesota 56002
www.stonearchbooks.com

Library of Congress Cataloging-in-Publication Data
Meister, Cari, 1955-
    Goalkeeper Goof / by Cari Meister; illustrated by Cori Doerrfeld.
    p. cm. — (My first graphic novel)
    ISBN 978-1-4342-1292-4 (library binding)
    ISBN 978-1-4342-1409-6 (pbk.)
    1. Graphic novels. [1. Graphic novels. 2. Soccer—Fiction.] I. Doerrfeld, Cori, ill.
I. Sullivan, Mary, 1958- ill. II. Title.
PZ7.7.M45Go 2009
741.5'973—dc22   2008031965

Summary: David likes soccer, but he doesn't like being goalie. When it's his
turn at the net, he tries a new trick. David is ready to even the score!

Art Director: Heather Kindseth
Graphic Designer: Hilary Wacholz

1 2 3 4 5 6 14 13 12 11 10 09

My **FIRST** Graphic Novel

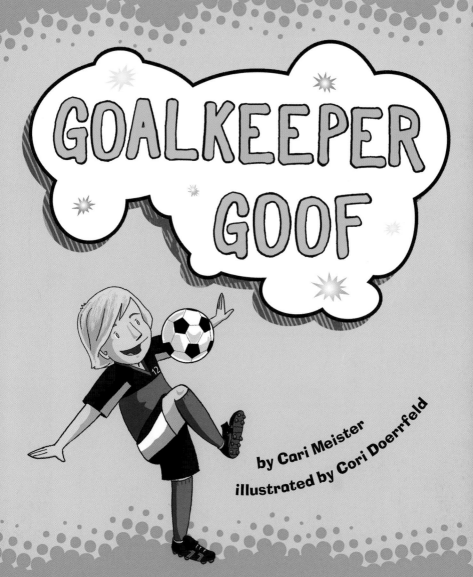

GOALKEEPER GOOF

by Cari Meister

illustrated by Cori Doerrfeld

STONE ARCH BOOKS
www.stonearchbooks.com

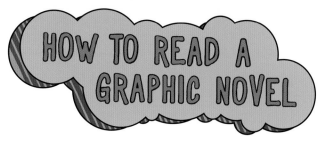

HOW TO READ A GRAPHIC NOVEL

Graphic novels are easy to read. Boxes called panels show you how to follow the story. Look at the panels from left to right and top to bottom.

Read the word boxes and word balloons from left to right as well. Don't forget the sound and action words in the pictures.

The pictures and the words work together to tell the whole story.

David pulled on his shin guards.

He tied the laces on his new cleats.

David frowned. He did not want
to go to the soccer game.

At the field, David's team warmed up.

They ran laps.

They dribbled the ball.

Good one!

They kicked the ball.

David liked to run. He liked to dribble. He liked to kick.

David was good at those activities.

David did not like to play goalkeeper. He always missed the ball. The other team always scored.

David's team called him the "Goalkeeper Goof."

He missed the ball again!

Oh no!

The first half of the game was great.
David did not play goalkeeper.

He ran.

He dribbled.

He passed the ball to Angel.

Angel scored!

Then David stole the ball.

He kicked.

He scored!

Yeah!

"Keep your eye on the ball," she said.
"Don't forget to use your hands."

David always forgot the part about using his hands. Then he had an idea.

David wiggled his fingers.

WIGGLE

That's it!

He ran to the goal. He
kept wiggling his fingers.

"It's the Goalkeeper Goof,"
said Angel.

David pretended not to hear.
He just kept wiggling his fingers.

David watched
the ball.

David wiggled his fingers. He was not going to forget to use his hands this time.

The ball was coming right at him!
He put up his hands. Then he
jumped as high as he could.

He caught the ball!
The game was over.

I did it!

David was no longer the Goalkeeper Goof! He was the Goalkeeper Champ!

You're the champ, David!

The End

ABOUT THE AUTHOR

Cari Meister is the author of many books for children, including the My Pony Jack series and *Luther's Halloween*. She lives on a small farm in Minnesota with her husband, four sons, three horses, one dog, and one cat. Cari enjoys running, snowshoeing, horseback riding, and yoga. She loves to visit libraries and schools.

ABOUT THE ILLUSTRATOR

Cori Doerrfeld has been drawing since she was a little girl. She always knew she would grow up to be an artist. After studying art and illustration in college, she began work as a children's book illustrator. Cori has illustrated several titles, including a picture book with actress Brooke Shields. When not hard at work painting, Cori enjoys spending time with her daughter, reading comics, and spending time outdoors.

cleats (kleetz)—shoes with spikes on the
bottom

dribbled (DRIB-uhld)—to move a soccer ball
forward by kicking it

goalkeeper (GOHL-keep-ur)—the player who
defends the goal

halftime (HAF-time)—the break in the middle
of the game

shin guard (shin gard)—a piece of sports
equipment that protects the shins

DISCUSSION QUESTIONS

1.) David did not like being teased. Have you ever been teased? If so, what did you do about it?

2.) David's coach believed in him. She knew he would be a good goalkeeper if he kept trying. Have you ever had a coach or a teacher help you with something? If so, what was it?

3.) David thinks of a special trick to help him remember to use his hands. Have you ever used a trick to remember something?

WRITING PROMPTS

1.) If you were the coach, what kind of warm-up would you create? Write down at least three warm-up activities. Then grab some friends and try them out.

2.) In the book, David has two nicknames. Write down some friendly nicknames for your friends and family.

3.) Throughout the book, there are sound and action words next to some of the art. Pick at least two of those words. Then write your own sentences using those words.

THE FIRST STEP INTO GRAPHIC NOVELS

My FIRST Graphic Novel

These books are the perfect introduction to the world of safe, appealing graphic novels. Each story uses familiar topics, repeating patterns, and core vocabulary words appropriate for a beginning reader. Combine the entertaining story with comic book panels, exciting action elements, and bright colors and a safe graphic novel is born.

WHAM!

My FIRST Graphic Novel

GOALKEEPER GOOF

by Cori Meister
illustrated by Cori Doerrfeld

My FIRST Graphic Novel

THE END ZONE

by Lori Mortensen
illustrated by Mary Sullivan

ST Graphic Novel

RAH-RAH RUBY!

by Christianne C. Jones
illustrated by Cori Doerrfeld

My FIRST Graphic Novel

T-BALL TROUBLE

by Cori Meister
illustrated by Jannie Ho

INTERNET SITES

Do you want to know more about subjects related to this book? Or are you interested in learning about other topics? Then check out FactHound, a fun, easy way to find Internet sites.

Our investigative staff has already sniffed out great sites for you!

Here's how to use FactHound:

1. Visit *www.facthound.com*

2. Select your grade level.

3. To learn more about subjects related to this book, type in the book's ISBN number: 1434212920.

4. Click the Fetch It button.

FactHound will fetch the best Internet sites for you!